Sammy and Mara

First published in Great Britain 1978
by Hamish Hamilton Children's Books Ltd.,
90, Great Russell Street, London WC1B 3PT
ISBN: 0 241 10024 0

Printed and bound in Great Britain by
Morrison & Gibb Ltd, London and Edinburgh

Sammy and Mara

Ron and Atie van der Meer

Hamish Hamilton · *London*

My name is Sammy. This is Siva
and the black and white cat is Sono.

My big sister Mara can talk. This is our Mummy
and that tall man is our Daddy.

Oh dear, Mara wants to pick me up again.
Playing with her usually ends in crying.

Mummy gives me a cuddle
and tells Mara not to carry me.

When Mara is jealous she asks for the potty
to get attention. It always takes ages.

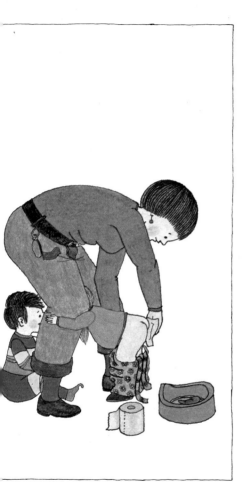  

At last she has finished. Daddy says Mara's a good girl.
When I do it Mummy says 'What a dirty nappy!'

Hooray, here's Grandma. Mummy tells Mara to say hello.

Is Mara going to kiss her? No! She wants Grandma's hat.

Grandma's reading us a story
but I'd rather play with Sono. Help!

We're going to post a letter. I like the rain
but I don't think Grandma and Mara do.

Mara wants to play doctor again. I don't like this game.

This looks better. I'll wait till she's finished, and then . . .

Mara is pulling leaves off in the garden.
Mummy says it hurts the plants.

Mara says sorry and kisses all the plants,
even an enormous big tree.

I have fun at mealtimes but Daddy thinks I'm messy.

Ridiculous. A big girl like Mara being fed by Mummy.

Ring-a-ring o' roses,
a pocket full of posies.

Atishoo! Atishoo!
We all fall down.

We are tigers and we're chasing Mara. Boo!

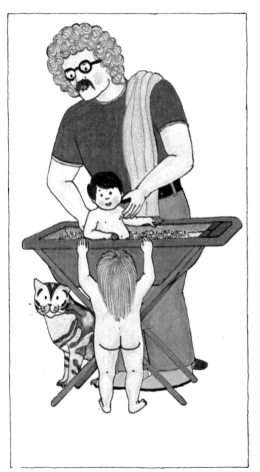

Bathtime's fun too. Sorry Daddy!
Mara's too big for my bath. Silly girl!

Mara wants her tooth brush.
I'm glad I haven't got any teeth yet.

Goodnight, Sammy.

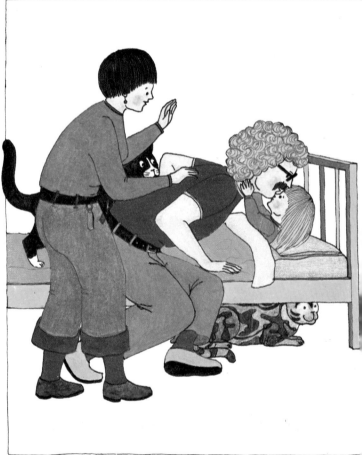

Goodnight, Mara.